amō ōsapotawan

AMŌ'S
Sapotawan

BOOK TWO IN THE SIX SEASONS SERIES

By William Dumas

Illustrated by Rhian Brynjolson

HIGHWATER
PRESS

Introduction

Sapotawana:
Rites of Passage.

◇◇◇

Generation after generation, the asiniskaw īthiniwak, the Rocky Cree, lived according to the cycle of the six seasons and thirteen moons. Each season posed unique challenges that tested the asiniskaw īthiniwak and required them to develop survival skills—physical, emotional, spiritual and mental.

One of the most important asiniskaw īthiniwak tools for survival is sapotawana: the rites of passage that acknowledge each person as they attain certain skill levels at particular stages of life. Sapotawana encourage people to discover their gifts, learn about their responsibilities, and find their life's purpose.

At each sapotawan, you are going through a metamorphosis, like many of our relatives the animals do. Think of a caterpillar turning into a butterfly, or a bird moulting so that its new wing feathers can grow in.

The first sapotawan occurs when a person enters this world. These rites of passage continue as you unfold through the different transitions of your life:

awasis, child; oskatis, young adult; kīhti aya, adult; and kisi amiya, an elder, the time of life when your work is done.

Sapotawana are there to guide each of us on our miskanaw, our path in life. Each sapotawan is acknowledged and celebrated by our minisiwin, our immediate family, as well as by our ototimīhītowin, our grandparents, aunts, uncles, and cousins, and our wāhkotowin, our adopted relatives.

Although the understanding of these rites of passage has changed over time, the underlying concept is still the same: celebrating a person's accomplishments as they go through life. Today we might think of advancing to the next grade level as a sapotawan, or graduating from school, getting married, or starting your first job.

Sapotawana recognize that you are always learning throughout different times of your life, and that you have new things to offer the world as you gain these skills.

ithinisakahikan

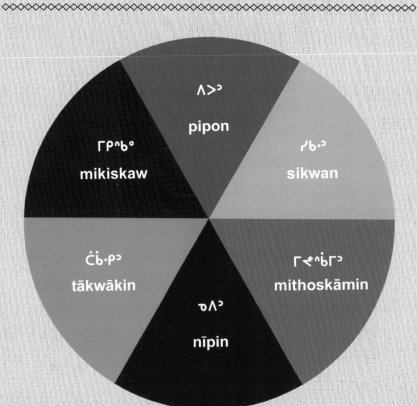

The Six Seasons of the Asiniskaw Īthiniwak series tells the stories of the asiniskaw īthiniwak (Rocky Cree) and their life on the land of what is now north-central Manitoba. These stories are set during the mid-1600s before direct contact with Europeans in this area. They seek to teach young people about the old ways. *Amō's Sapotawan* is set in nīpin.

Nīpin, or summer, translates to "gifts from the water" (nipi = water; in = to give) because this is the season of the raspberry rains followed by the blueberry rains. The moons for this season are paskahawī pīsim (egg hatching moon) and paskowī pīsim (moulting moon). Paskowī pīsim happens in midsummer when all the birds lose their flying feathers. At this time, the birds are not hunted. They are raising their young. The asiniskaw īthiniwak fish, gather berries and medicine, and make pottery and baskets during this time.

In this book, you will learn about Amō's sapotawan as she is recognized for her skill as a pottery maker. You'll see how her minisiwin uses the community's kakānohkimowina, their guiding principles, to help prepare her for this metamorphosis. There are also other sapotawana spread throughout this story. See which ones you can find, and imagine which sapotawana you might aim toward as you ponder your own miskanaw.

Story Characters

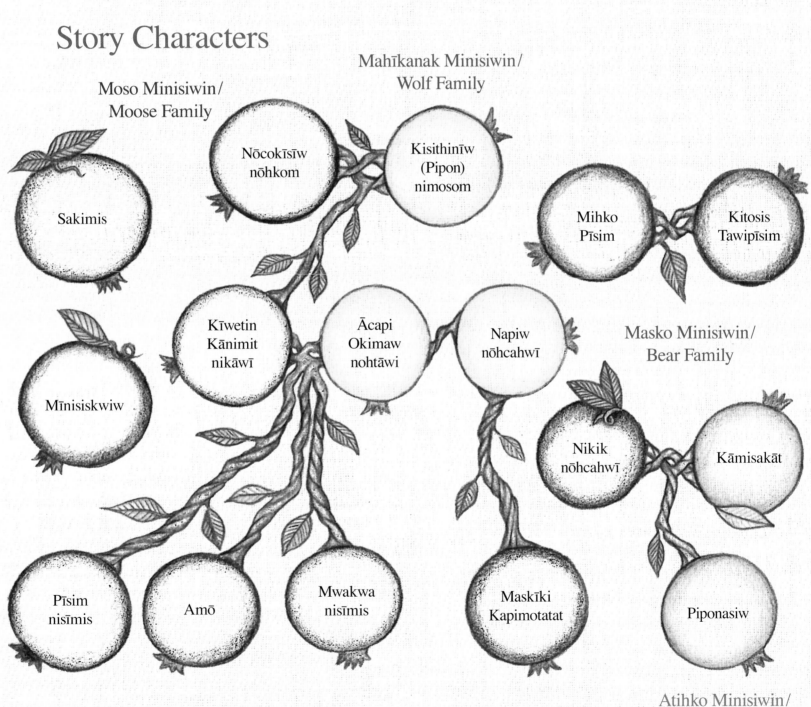

Moso Minisiwin/
Moose Family

Mahīkanak Minisiwin/
Wolf Family

Nōcokīsīw
nōhkom

Kisithinīw
(Pipon)
nimosom

Sakimis

Mihko
Pīsim

Kitosis
Tawipīsim

Kīwetin
Kānimit
nikāwī

Ācapi
Okimaw
nohtāwi

Napiw
nōhcahwī

Masko Minisiwin/
Bear Family

Mīnisiskwiw

Nikik
nōhcahwī

Kāmisakāt

Pīsim
nisīmis

Amō

Mwakwa
nisīmis

Maskīki
Kapimotatat

Piponasiw

Atihko Minisiwin/
Caribou Family

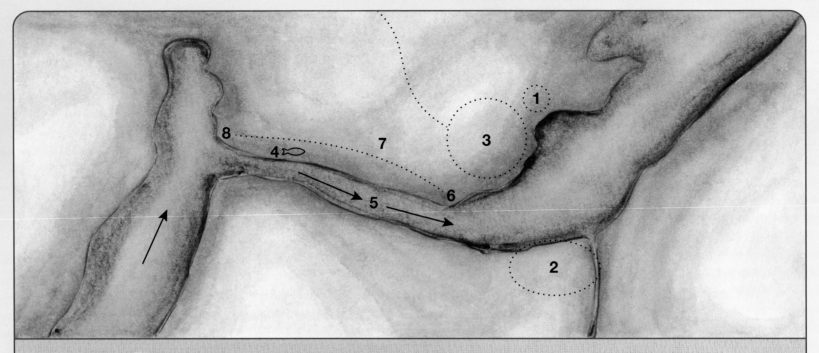

mikisiwaci (Eagle Hill)

1. wapatanask (clay pit)
2. apiscithīnīwak (the place of the little people)
3. wikinanaski (campsite)
4. picipothakan (fish weir)
5. mikisiwi pawīstik (Eagle Rapids)
6. kapawin (boat landing place)
7. onikāhp (portage)
8. posiwin (leaving place)

Kayās, kapi mana niki papamacihonan tāhtwaw kakwiskayawahk patos iti niki ayanan iwithotak ita tapimacihisowak. Piyākwaw imikwa nīpihk mikisiwi pawistik niki misakanan ikiniti notamithikiyak akwa ikiniti mawisoyak. Kwayask kimithowitakwan mina kipapiyāhtakan.

Long time ago we moved from place to place with the seasonal changes. We would travel to different areas to harvest the food that was available at each season. One time, it was nīpin, midsummer, when we arrived by canoe at mikisiwi pawistik, Eagle Rapids, to harvest fish and to pick berries. It was so enjoyable and peaceful there – a time of plenty.

The thunderbirds had
arrived, bringing with
them the roaring thunder and lightning
but also the raspberry rains. It had cooled
off now, and the athoskanak, the raspberries,
had begun to ripen. In the evening air, Amō sat
at the mouth of mikisiwi pawistik, repeating to
herself the name of the moon that she had been taught,
"paskowī pīsim, paskowī pīsim." This was the moulting
moon, when the waterfowl dropped their feathers and
grew new ones.

The water was ītōmikathwāstik, mirror calm. Amō quickly
looked around to see if anybody was watching her.
No one was, so she looked down into her reflection

THUNDERBIRDS

Thunderbirds represent powerful forces in asiniskaw īthiniwak culture, manifested in many aspects of the natural world, for example, in thunderstorms and lightning strikes. The appearance of the Thunderbirds marks the beginning of particular activities on the land. When the Thunderbirds are heard in the spring, it is the signal for people to pick medicine plants. They also take their medicine bundles out to have them blessed by the Thunderbirds. Later in the season, the Thunderbirds signal the beginning of the ripening periods and the start of the forest fire season.

OLD SONGS AND NEW SONGS

Songs are important for capturing and carrying family and group history. There are many songs that have been handed down through the generations. Songs also come to people from the spirit world or as they observe the land and each other. The land carries the rhythm of the language. The children of the asiniskaw īthiniwak learn this rhythm through song, beginning with the lullabies sung to them as infants. Songs are often accompanied by a mitihikan, a hand drum that represents the beating of the heart. Singers have the important role of moving people forward on their miskanaw, their life's path.

CREE VOCABULARY

ītōmikathwāstik: mirror calm. Ītōmi means calm and wāstik means shining.

apiscithīnīwak: little people. As explained in the Six Seasons book *The Gift of the Little People*, there are two other kinds of little people. The apiscithīnīwak are exact replicas of us humans, except much smaller. The word comes from apisci (small) and īnīwak (human beings).

MWAKWA'S EVENING SONG

	[English Translation]
achahko pimotihōwin	
miskanaw nipimotan	
tapwisa mithawasin	Spirit travelling,
achahko pimotihōwin	I'm on my journey.
miskanaw nipimotan	It is so beautiful.
māskīkīy inataman	Spirit travelling,
	I'm on my journey.
māskīkīy inataman	
kitwam nitotimak tamithwayacik	I go to gather medicine.
akwa	I go to gather medicine
makoko nitotimak kakinikanoticik	so that my family
ipinaci nakiskawicik	will be well again.
ipapimotiyak	
ipapapiyak mina	Here come my relatives
iyacimoyak	those who went ahead of us
kayās mana oci	coming to meet me halfway.
tapwisa mithwasin	We walk together,
omahita katakosinan	we laugh together
ititho ipiyatakak	and we tell stories
ikotahota māskīkīy	that happened long ago.
tapimatisimakak	
kayās ikiyapatak	It is so beautiful
kiyam maka nakiwan	where we've arrived.
nakiwitatan oma	It is so peaceful here
māskīkīy nitotimak	where the medicine lives
ipipapimotiya achahko	that was used long ago.
pimotihōwin	
miskanaw inikamoyan	It's all right now, I'll go home.
	I will take this medicine
WI OH HI HI OH HI OH HI	for my relatives.
OH HI OH HI OH HI OH HI OH HI	I walk the spirit-traveling path
OH HI OH HI	as I sing.
WI OH HI OH HI OH HI OH HI OH	
HI OH WI HI OH	
HI OH HI OH HI HO HI	WI OH HI HI OH HI OH HI
	OH HI OH HI OH HI
achahko pimotihōwin	OH HI OH HI OH HI OH HI
miskanaw nipimotan	WI OH HI OH HI OH
tapwisa mithawasin	HI OH HI OH HI OH
	WI HI OH
	HI OH HI OH HI HO HI

---

in the water and grinned. "Wow, I don't look like a little girl anymore!" she said to herself, remembering that she would soon be in her fourteenth winter.

Further along the shore she could hear her brother Mwakwa starting to beat his drum and sing the evening song. She always loved the songs that Mwakwa sang. He had such a beautiful energetic voice. Some of the songs the minisiwin sang had been passed on from generation to generation, and new ones were being made all the time. As she listened, Amō looked across the river at the rock face that jutted out of the water. The old people had often told stories about the apiscithīnīwak, the little people, who lived on the other side of the rock. It would be so nice if she could just walk over there to visit them.

"Amō! Amō! Pikiwi akwa! Pikiwi akwa! Amō, come home now!" It was her mom, Kīwitin Kānimit, Northwind Dancing, pulling Amō out of her daydream. She remembered she had been sent to get the water for the evening māskīkīwapwiy, the evening medicine tea. She stood up and picked up her two askihkwak, clay pots, and started walking up the hill. On her way to the top, where their summer mikiwāhp had been set up for a good vantage point, she met Maskīki Kapimotatat, Medicine Carrier, coming up from the river holding an armful of wihkaskwa, mint, for their tea. Maskīki Kapimotatat had the gift of finding aski māskīkīya, herbal plants for medicine, tea, and food. She was always wandering away by herself, searching for and picking the various aski māskīkīya that were available for cures and māskīkīwapwiy.

SUMMER MIKIWĀHP

Summer dwellings, mikiwāhp, are temporary shelters, set up when and where needed, for example, during travel. People build a framework of poles, large saplings, or branches and cover this with pieces of bark in summer, animal hides in winter, or whatever else is available. Winter dwellings are similar, but sturdier and more long-lasting.

ASKIHKWAK

Askihkwak, pottery vessels, were made in northern Manitoba by pre-contact Indigenous people, who combined clay and water with fine rocks or sand (temper) to produce vessels that were fired and became useful artistic items. The first pots were made during the Middle Woodland period (about 2500–1000 years ago) and were cone-shaped, with a smoothed exterior and many complex decorations. During the Late Woodland period (about 1000–150 years ago), when Amō lived, people made pottery with rounded bases in fabric bags, with minimal decoration. This globular shape made the pot stable on flat surfaces and within the hot coals of a kotawān, a fire. People also used these vessels to store food and carry things.

MASKĪHKIYA

Knowledge of the gift of medicines, maskīhkiya, is passed on within families. Children are observed in the first few years of life, and those who are drawn to medicines become those chosen to carry that gift. Medicine people start their training in maskīhkiya early in life, with their gifts nurtured by close family members and other medicine carriers. Along with wihkaskwa (wild mint), the medicines that are harvested at this time in asiniskaw īthiniwak territory include ithinimina (blueberries), wīkis (rat root), waskatamo (water lily root), and aski askatask (cow parsnip).

CREE VOCABULARY

māskīkīwapwiy: medicine tea.

aski māskīkīya: land medicine. Every plant used as medicine is taken from the land. When you eat an animal, you are eating the medicines the animal ate.

wihkaskwa: mint tea.

9

Amō got to the top of the hill and
stopped to look at the sunset unfolding
before her. It was always a gift to
watch. Kāmīkwaskwak, the reddish
colour, was breathtaking, spread out
along the whole horizon. She took
a deep breath and exhaled,
marveling at how it
brought so much calm
to everyone.

She entered the
mikiwāhp, put
her water down,
and walked
over to the
askihk where
māskihkiwapwiy
had been made.

She smelled the warm, spicy aroma as she dipped her birchbark cup into the māskihkiwapwiy and then sipped, savouring the beautiful medicine that gives life. The askihk was nearly empty now, so she added some of her isohkistitat, fresh water, into the māskīkīwapwiy over the fire, to reboil it for the next batch of medicine.

BIRCHBARK CUPS

Birchbark cups are made by waterproofing a small birchbark container using a special tar. This tar is made by distilling the natural gum found in birchbark. The bark is packed into a fireproof container with a hole in the bottom, resting atop another fireproof container. The two containers are placed in the ground with hot coals. As the bark heats up, it excretes a resin that collects in the lower container and creates the tar that is used to coat utensils such as cups to make them waterproof.

LONG SUMMER DAYS AND SUNSETS

At the latitude of South Indian Lake (56.7807° N), the day at summer solstice is 17 hours and 50 minutes long. The sun rises at 4:42 a.m. and goes down at 10:32 p.m. Amō's story takes place during the Moulting Moon, two moons after the summer solstice, when days are becoming shorter. But, even at this time of the summer, the day has close to 15 hours of sunlight between 6 a.m. and 9 p.m.

CREE VOCABULARY

kāmīkwaskwak: the reddish-coloured sky at sunset. Mīkwa means red and waskō is the cloud. When the sky is reddish in the evening, it means there is good calm weather coming the next day.

11

Her mother sat down beside her. "Amō, from the time you were a little girl, you've always enjoyed making things with your hands. Kōhcawī Nikik, your uncle, has offered to show you how to make nipisiwata, willow baskets—he makes such beautiful baskets. Kōhkom Nōcokīsīw, your grandmother, has offered to show you how to make kwakwāywata, birchbark baskets, and containers and plates. Since you were a little girl you have also enjoyed making things with clay. You've already learned how to make little askihkwak. Your auntie, kitosis Tawipīsim, Sun Breaking Through the Clouds, has offered to begin your apprenticeship with her to make askihkwak and weave the bags for the askihkwak. Soon you will be entering your sapotawan to choose which skill you want to master."

Amō crawled into her bed, and as she was falling asleep, she imagined herself someday mastering her mīthikowisiwin, her gift. But what would her mīthikowisiwin be? How would she know what was right for her?

APPRENTICESHIP

Children are born with innate gifts necessary for survival and for contributing to the community, but children and their parents are also responsible for developing these gifts. Children are expected to learn by listening to stories and observing their environment and the actions of those around them. Babies are often put in swings and cradleboards so they can observe those around them. When old enough, children choose one of their gifts, a mīthikowisiwin, to master by becoming an apprentice to someone in the community. At first, children are not given verbal instructions but are expected to observe until they are able to properly visualize what is being done. Then, when they are ready, a teacher invites them to try to imitate what the teacher does. As they practice, the child experiments with different ways of doing things. This is a hands-on, practical approach to learning, focused on understanding and interacting with the surrounding environment, until mastery is achieved.

BIRCH BASKETS

Kwakwāywata, birch baskets, are used to carry food, hold water, and store items. The first step to making a basket is to carefully remove a long, thin piece of bark encircling a birch tree with a sharp knife, usually in late spring, so that the tree has time to recover in the summer. The outer bark is then removed from these thin pieces and flattened. Bark can be cut in various shapes, depending on the type of basket that is required. A sharp awl tool (made of wood, stone, or bone) is used to make holes in the birchbark after it has been bent into shape. Lastly, spruce roots or other fibres are used as thread to sew the basket together. These fibres are cleaned and soaked to make them more pliable, so that pieces of birchbark will hold together in different shapes of baskets.

FIBRE BAGS

Globular-shaped vessels, made during Amō's time, were manufactured inside woven bags made of twisted plant fibres, bags that could also be used for carrying items. We know that this was the method used because the negative impression of the bag is preserved on the exteriors of many pottery sherds or pieces. Unique to Amō's region, some pots also have fabric impressions on the *interior*. It took countless hours to collect, process, and then twist willow or cedar fibres together into a fine textile bag. These articles undoubtedly were cherished items after they were crafted. Since they were made from organic materials, they are not preserved in archaeological sites in the boreal forest.

CREE VOCABULARY

mīthikowisiwina: the gifts you are given. Mīthi means to give, and kowisiwin means a constant movement toward mastery. Mīthikowisiwina refers especially to your talents and potential. Children are born with four gifts, and it is up to parents and teachers to help the children develop those gifts so that they can aim toward mastering them. There is never a full mastery since you always keep learning, but, if you dedicate yourself, you will eventually have enough mastery to become a teacher for the next generation.

CLAY PIT

For thousands of years, people around the world have used clay to make pots and other items. Potters search for clay with the right characteristics. Such deposits can be rare, and good locations are revisited. In Amō's time, suitable clay was dug up, cleaned of plant roots and rocks, pounded, and mixed with water to test its quality. Potters then mixed the clay with pulverized rock, sand, or other temper to improve its ability to maintain a shape. This step also helped release steam from the clay to reduce breakage during firing. The knowledge needed to achieve the right vessel form requires experience built over a lifetime.

MAKING FISH SPEARS

Fish spearheads were carved from animal bone or antler and then combined with wood for a shaft and hafting material to hold them all together. These were then decorated with feathers, paint, or other embellishments. Fish spears used to capture smaller fish on small rivers and in pihcipothākana, fish weirs, were hand-held tools thrust quickly to catch fish and then lift them up into a canoe or onto the riverbank. A specific kind of spear for catching larger fish is a harpoon. Harpoons had barbed spearheads comprised of two long, jagged edges that would catch the slippery fish in the water. The harpoon head was linked on a long line to the shaft, so that, if it detached from the shaft, it would not be lost.

Early the next morning Amō woke up to the sound of the wasipistān, the morning lark, singing, "Pitapan. Light is coming." It was soon followed by the robin's song, "Kinanāskomitin, opimācihiwiw kāpimacihiyin. I thank you Creator for giving me life." She crawled out of her warm robes and walked down to the river to wash and groom her hair. When she came back into the mikiwāhp, her mother had already set māskihkiwapwiy for her to drink and food to begin her day. Kīwitin Kānimit and Tawipīsim were sitting by the kotawān, the fire, drinking their share of māskihkiwapwiy, telling each other stories, with teasing and laughter between the stories.

When breakfast was done, Amō and Tawipīsim walked down to the clay pit and started taking what they would need for the day's work.

The men were out at mikisiwi pawistik, harvesting the pickerel at the fish weir that had been made such a long time ago. Amō's aunt Kāmisakāt, Kīwitin Kānimit, Nōcokīsīw and a couple of iskwīsisak, young girls, were helping to dress the fish and make the kinosiwi pimī, the fish oil, which was stored in jackfish containers.

Mīnisiskwiw, Maskīki Kapimotatat, Pīsim, and the smaller iskwīsisak were out on the hills picking athoskanak, raspberries. Nōhcawī Nikik was in his usual spot overlooking two sides of the lake, watching for visitors who might come to the camp. Today he was also making arrowheads and fish spears.

FISH OIL AND CONTAINERS

Fish oil is made by boiling fish guts. The fat from the guts melts and forms an oil on top of the water, which is then skimmed off and stored. Pimiwāta, fish oil containers, can be made from fish intestines or opahkwaci, the swim bladder. Jackfish can be made into containers by removing the head, hollowing out the fish's insides, filling the cavity with oil, and hanging the fish container to dry. Filling the container with oil immediately after it is made prevents it from shriveling as it dries.

FISH WEIR

Pihcipothākana, fish weirs, are structures used to trap fish in shallow, narrow, and calm waters. They are constructed in different ways depending on specific river conditions. Taking advantage of natural rock formations or bays, pihcipothākana can span the width of a river. Large sticks or logs and rocks are set into the river bottom at an angle to create a fence that allows for the flow of water but not the passage of fish. Building pihcipothākana is a lot of work, but they allow fishers to stand in the water, grab the trapped fish, and throw them to shore.

In all this busy time, Amō gazed upward and noticed she could look directly at the sun, which was a big red ball in the sky. "Nikāwī, Mom, look! Why does the sky look like that?" Kīwitin Kānimit looked up and said, "Nitānis, my girl, it is the season when thunder and lightning come, and the lightning starts forest fires. Look in the distance at that big plume of smoke that's rising. It is the smoke, high up in the sky, that makes the sun look like that. We have to keep an eye on iti kapasitihk, that forest fire. Kwiskītīkī, if the wind turns, it will quickly burn towards us and we'll be in trouble. For now, we are safe."

BLAZE ORANGE SUN

A sun that looks blaze-orange is a sign that there is a large amount of smoke in the air from a forest fire. Even when flames or smoke plumes are not clearly visible, natural signs such as this indicate danger and the need to keep an eye out. Learning to observe and interpret what is taking place in the surrounding landscape is an important skill for life on the land. Signs in nature may serve as warnings, foretell the weather, or indicate what plants are safe to eat or use as medicine.

FOREST FIRES

A natural part of a forest's lifecycle, fires renew plant life. Often caused by lightning strikes, they can also be intentionally set by humans in isolated areas, such as meadows and islands, in the springtime when the ground is still wet and cold. When done correctly, these environments can be burned with little risk of fire spreading beyond the chosen location. Such burns lead to the growth of wild berries and other plants that attract animals such as moose, who will raise their young in these areas. Controlled fires can also be used to create meadow lands for campsites. During Amō's time, the frequency and location of lightning strikes allowed people to predict the locations of forest fires, which were often allowed to run their course. While considered a blessing in renewing the forest, fires were also understood to be dangerous. They could spread against the wind, over the tops of trees, or even through the root systems. Quickly spreading fires sometimes caught people off guard, and they would then try to take refuge on rivers or islands.

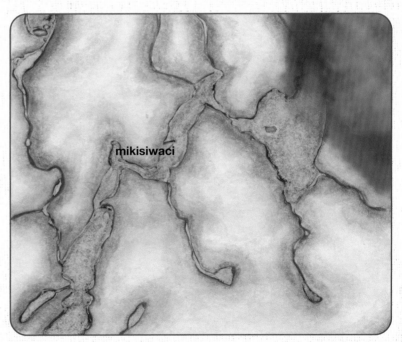

mikisiwaci

The smoke indicates the direction of the approaching forest fire.

CREE VOCABULARY

kwiskītīkī: if the wind turns.

itī kāpasitīk: a forest fire is there. The root word is pasitī, fire, and kā means "it's right there."

From the direction of mikisiwi pawistik, the canoes came shooting down the fast current, and, at the perfect moment, the men leaned on their paddles to swing their canoes to the shore. Then they started throwing the morning's catch onto the pile of spruce boughs that had been laid there to keep the fish clean. Nōcokīsīw surveyed the morning's catch. "We have a lot of fish already. Anoc ka nipihk, this summer, the harvest has been good. We have enough to smoke, dry, and pound into flakes. We already have a few kwakwāywata full, and we have many jackfish containers of fish oil. We should be done this harvest by tomorrow." The men came to the kotawān and started eating their midday meal of roasted atīhkamik, whitefish.

Ācapi Okimaw told the story of the other day at niciwām pawistik, Brotherly Love Rapids. Napiw, Mihko Pīsim, Nikik, and Ācapi Okimaw had gone there to fish with the spears that Nikik had made, and Napiw speared a big sturgeon. Ācapi Okimaw started teasing his big brother. "That huge sturgeon just about pulled Napiw into the current! It took all four of us to fight it and bring it to shore."

SHOOTING RAPIDS

The most important thing to do when shooting rapids is to stop and check the rapids first. Skillful canoeists read the rapids so that they know exactly where to go. When they shoot the rapids, the otakwahamo, the person in the back of the canoe, and the onistamokiw, the person in the front of the canoe, need to be in very good communication with one another. They also need to trust one another.

PROCESSING AND PRESERVING FISH

Processing and preserving fish for later consumption was an important task of the summer and fall seasons. There were many ways this could be done depending on the type of fish. Some fish were pounded and mixed with dry berries to create pīmikan, a highly nutritious food that resembles a cake or type of jerky and which could also be made with other forms of meat. Some fish were filleted, skewered on a wooden stick, and cooked over the fire, a style of cooking known as apwanask. Some fish were smoked by hanging them in an akwayan, a tent with a fire fueled by rotten wood that creates a lot of smoke. Some fish were pounded to create fish flakes. Once processed, the fish was stored in various caches to eat in the winter. Other parts of the fish were also used to create items like fish oil for long-term use.

STURGEON

Sturgeon are among the largest and strongest freshwater fish in the misinipi (Churchill River) drainage area. Catching sturgeon required specialized hooks, spears, and nets. These hooks have been found in several places in Rocky Cree territory, some of them dating back to ancient times.

HARVEST ONLY ENOUGH TO SUSTAIN US

A guiding principle for the asiniskaw īthiniwak of living sustainably on the land was and is to only take only enough of a resource to sustain the needs of the community. For example, when pihcipothākana are used, once enough fish are caught, the remaining fish are released to avoid overharvesting. When hunting moose, nursing female moose with calves are usually left alone, if the hunter has a choice. This helps to ensure that there will be moose, fish, and other animals left to sustain the people in the future. When plant resources such as birchbark are needed, only what is needed for the project at hand is taken in order to preserve enough trees with bark for future use. The asiniskaw īthiniwak use various ways to express their respect and thanks to the plants and animals that sustain them.

"Nikik always makes good tools that provide for us," Kāmisakāt said. "He told me that before they left niciwām pawistik, he lifted the moss high and put one of his prized fish hooks there as an offering of thanks for that gift. Because of my husband's skills, tonight we are having sturgeon for our day's end meal." Napiw looked around at the fish harvest. "We have always made sure we only gather enough to sustain us, and, once we have enough, we move to the next camp. Nōcokīsīw says that we will be done here by tomorrow. That's good! We also have to be watchful of the fire in the distance. Kwiskītīkī, it will come our way very fast."

"Amō, fill an askihk with water and take it up to the berry pickers and kōcawi Nikik. They'll need a drink soon," Kīwitin Kānimit said to her daughter. Amō did as she was told, carrying her askihk up the hill. She thought about the skills needed to be a berry picker and how some people loved to pick berries. She twitched her nose and muttered to herself, "That's not me. I'm not a berry picker. I'd rather be making things."

While she was thinking aloud to herself, she looked up the hill and saw a huge kakītiwi maskwa, a black bear, coming towards the water between her and the berry pickers. Amō wanted to call out to Nikik, but he was busy with his work, and anyway her voice wouldn't come out. The maskwa kept coming toward her, away from the berry pickers. All of a sudden, the maskwa realized that someone was close to him, and he came crashing right towards Amō. Charging!

Instinctively, she remembered what otawīya, her dad, once told her: if a maskwa charges, do not run. Stand still. Just freeze. She held her breath and clenched her mouth to stop herself from screaming. And when the maskwa was only a few feet from her, it suddenly turned aside and kept running down the hill, along its original path.

Amō was still frozen. She started walking, but her legs gave out on her, and she had to grab a young poplar to hold herself up. That was when she realized her hands were empty. She had dropped her askihk. She looked back and saw the broken pieces spread out on the ground where she had been standing.

CLOSE ENCOUNTERS WITH BEARS

Bertha's Story, as told by William Dumas

A lady once shared a story with me about the time she spent at a cabin on the Churchill River with her baby daughter. Sometimes, in the summertime, you leave the door open, to let the cool air in from the lake. That's what she did. But then a bear came along and walked right in the cabin door! It was a good thing the cabin had rafters. She had seen the bear walking by the window, and so she grabbed the baby and climbed up there, and she hung onto those rafters the whole time the bear looked around. Finally, it went back outside without hurting anything. She said the bear never even noticed she was there.

Buckwheat's Story, as told by William Dumas

One summer I went to visit my family in South Indian Lake, and my brother called and said, "Come on over; I want to show you something." So I went over, and as soon as I got there he showed me the little orphan bear cub they had brought home. He said to his son, "Hey Buckwheat, come here, do that thing you do with the bear cub." So Buckwheat says okay, and he walks over to the little bear and they start a wrestling match. That little bear was very strong for his size! Buckwheat wrestled him for a few minutes, but pretty soon he got too tired. The bear cub never tried to hurt him.

Krystalyn's Story, as told by Krystalyn Harms

When I was around five or six years old, I always had a hard time remembering which way to put my shoes on. I kept putting my shoes on the opposite foot. I remember my mom would tell me, "Make sure to put your shoes on the right feet, or else you'll meet up with a bear!" Well one day we were driving from Split Lake to Thompson for a day trip, my parents and my sisters and I. Again, I had my shoes on the wrong feet. Then, all of a sudden we met up with a huge bear—we almost hit it! And once they stopped the car, my parents asked us, "Who has their shoes on backwards!?" I got scared and tried hiding my feet to not get caught, but they looked anyway and found out it was me! I immediately put my shoes on the right way. I learned my lesson that day.

"ALWAYS MOVE FORWARD"

This asiniskaw īthiniwak teaching says that, when you experience loss, you must not become too focused on what has been lost—instead you need to keep moving forward on your miskanaw. Even when someone dies, it is important to honour them by moving forward and not becoming trapped in grief. When Ācapi Okimaw tells Amō to take another askihk up the hill, he is teaching her to move forward instead of feeling bad about the broken one.

Finally, she regained her balance and walked back to the camp.

"Amō, you're back so early," her mother said. "What happened?"

"I met a maskwa, nikāwī! I was so scared that I dropped my askihk."

Ācapi Okimaw calmly looked at his daughter and said, "Get another askihk, Amō. Carry it back up the hill. They must be thirsty up there by now." It is the way of the asiniskaw īthiniwak: always move forward.

Amō walked cautiously up the hill, looking around constantly to
see if the maskwa might come back. When she got to Nikik and the
berry pickers, she offered them the water and sat beside her sister. "Pīsim,"
she whispered, "I tried to come up here once already, but a maskwa charged
me! I got so scared I broke my askihk, and I had to go and get another one.
But I made it back; I'm here!"

Pīsim laughed. "Oh Amō, you're a brave girl. It's a good thing that maskwa
didn't attack you. We wouldn't have had any water to drink." All of the berry
pickers started laughing, and Amō laughed with them.

After a while, she walked down the hill, not quite so worried about meeting
the maskwa again. When she was having her midday meal, Tawipīsim walked
up to her."I heard you broke the askihk when you met the maskwa, Amō. But
remember that you know how to make new askihkwak. Today, kasaskahānawak,
we will fire the pots, the ones we made two days ago."

Suddenly Amō understood the sign she had been given. This was her proud
day. Now she knew she would be a pottery maker.

THE ASINISKAW ĪTHINIWAK CREATION STORY AND POTTERY

Pottery is connected to the asiniskaw īthinwak creation story because the creation story is about the beginning of the land, which is what pottery vessels are made from. In the Cree word for pottery, askhikwak, the prefix "aski" means land or earth. Making pottery involves bringing together the four elements—water, earth, fire, and air—to create something new. It's a miniature version of the way everything was created and a reminder that all things come from the land. When someone works the land and receives gifts from the land, this is called "taking in medicine." All good things are thought of as medicine. Medicine is used to feed people, and gathering medicine from the land and using it to create new things is thought of as a labour of love. Pottery can be a form of medicine because it is used as a vessel from which to eat and drink. The asiniskaw īthiniwak express their reverence for the source of pottery, humans, and everything: the land.

CREE VOCABULARY

kasaskahānawak: We will fire up the pottery. Saska means to light a fire. Kasaskahānawak refers to the process in which the clay is hardened by placing it in a specially prepared fire.

wapatānask is the general word for clay.

wathaman is the ideal kind of clay for making pots, after temper has been added to the clay to make the pot hold together better.

That evening, the men returned from the mikisiwi pawistik fish harvest. Amō loved to watch how the canoes came out of the rapids toward the camp, pulling in smoothly to the calmer water where the men could unload them. Today, in one of the canoes she saw īwīthinohīt, a skinned black bear. The men acknowledged that this was Amō's maskwa. It had come out into the open after running from her, which had allowed the men to harvest it. Napiw said, "The bear robe will keep Amō warm this winter, the meat we will share amongst us, and we will have lots of bear grease for medicine and for our meals."

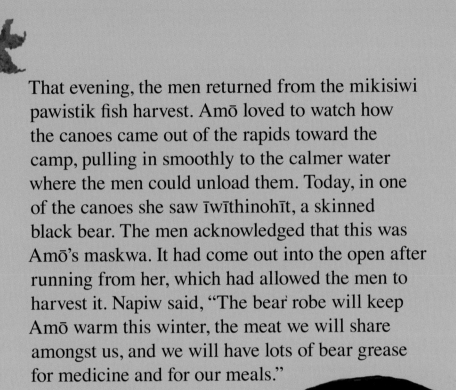

CEREMONIAL TREATMENT OF HUNTED BEARS

Bears and other hunted animals sacrifice themselves to hunters they deem worthy. To acknowledge this sacrifice, hunters treat these animals with the greatest respect and care by following strict rules. Many of these rules depend on the animal and the family or clan to which the hunter belongs. Generally speaking, hunters will thank the animal for giving them life, often by offering tobacco, and will properly dispose of the parts of the animal that are not taken to camp or are left over after eating. The hunter follows different rules for different parts of the animal. For example, animal bones and other leftovers should be returned to the earth in a clean area. If a hunter does not show respect by following the rules, animals will avoid them, and that hunter will not be successful.

BEARS AND MEDICINE

The bear is called maskwa, which is connected to the word māskīkīy, medicine, so the bear's name can be interpreted as, "you carry the medicine." That is why the bear is so well respected among the asiniskaw īthiniwak. There is medicine in the bear's fat, which is used as a moisturizer for people's hair and skin. It can also be used to treat rashes and other ailments. Some people are gifted with the ability to use the bear's hide and other parts of the bear in healing ceremonies.

CREE VOCABULARY

īwīthinohīt: A sacred ceremony of preparing the bear so that you are not wasting meat or fat from it. The bear has powerful medicines and must be treated with great respect. The word wīthin means fat. In hunter's language, a "dressed black bear" refers to a skinned, gutted, and quartered bear. Quartering is also dependent on size; some animals are so large that they have to be field-butchered and cut into smaller pieces before transportation.

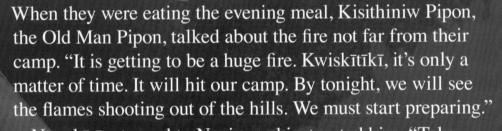

When they were eating the evening meal, Kisithiniw Pipon, the Old Man Pipon, talked about the fire not far from their camp. "It is getting to be a huge fire. Kwiskītīkī, it's only a matter of time. It will hit our camp. By tonight, we will see the flames shooting out of the hills. We must start preparing."

Nōcokīsīw turned to Napiw and instructed him, "Take three canoes and load up all the food that has been harvested. Take it to the middle of kinosi sākahīkan, Fish Lake. There's a place to keep the food cold over there for the next little while. Then make tisipicikana, caches, to hang up the smoked fish and fish flakes. We are going to be heading there anyway for the atīhkamik run after we are done here. Take the berries too. Many have been harvested, but there will be many more where we are going." She turned to the other women. "Tomorrow morning, as soon as we've had our morning meal, start packing our belongings and take them to the river's edge. We will take our mikiwāhpa down too. All the mikiwāhpa will be set close to the shore and, if need be, everything can quickly be loaded into the canoes when the men return and we can move to safety."

CACHES FOR SMOKED FISH

Foods such as smoked fish and other preserved meats can be stored long-term in food caches where they can be kept cold and dry. Within these caches, food is kept in waterproof bags made from loon skins or in baskets made of birchbark. One common type of food cache is made by digging a hole in the ground deep enough to reach the permafrost, approximately two to four feet deep. A floor made of spruce boughs is placed in these holes to prevent any heat generated by storing food from melting the permafrost and creating moisture. The holes are then covered with moss, creating a secure environment that can keep food cool indefinitely. Natural caverns can also be used as food caches in much the same way. In the wintertime, caches are constructed on raised platforms held up by stilts and covered in hides to keep frozen food safe from birds, dogs, and other animals.

HARVESTING BERRIES

Berries ripen and are picked at different times of the year, mostly from late summer into fall. Strawberries are the first to ripen, then raspberries and blueberries; by fall the cranberries ripen. Occasionally, cranberries that have not been found by humans or animals earlier are even picked in winter. During Amō's time, berries were dried and stored in birchbark baskets. Dried and pounded berries were also mixed with dried whitefish to make thiwahikānik, a kind of pīmikan made of fish.

Early the next morning, Kisithiniw moved from mikiwāhp to mikiwāhp calling, "Wāniska! Wāniska! Get up! The wind has shifted, and the fire is making its way to our camp. The smoke will be upon us soon and we will have a hard time breathing. Pack all our belongings and food. Move everything across the portage to the other side, to the mouth of mikisiwi pawistik. Take the canoes across the portage and wait. I'll be right there."

When the women and children got all the canoes and their belongings to the other side, they sat down to watch for the men's return from kinosi sākahīkan. The fire was getting closer and closer. Amō turned to her mom. "Nikāwī, all our beautiful askihkwak are going to be burned." Her mom looked at her and smiled. "Amō, we can make new askihkwak. We cannot make new lives." Amō was comforted.

The day was getting late. Nōcokīsīw stood up and looked back towards their old camp. "The fire has reached our place. You can hear the flames crackling. It will be here before too long."

Amō looked at her mom with panic. "Nikāwī, what are we going to do if the fire gets here?"

Her mom answered, "We will load the little ones into the canoe and get them away from danger. Some of us will wade into the river and pray that the smoke and fire don't get us."

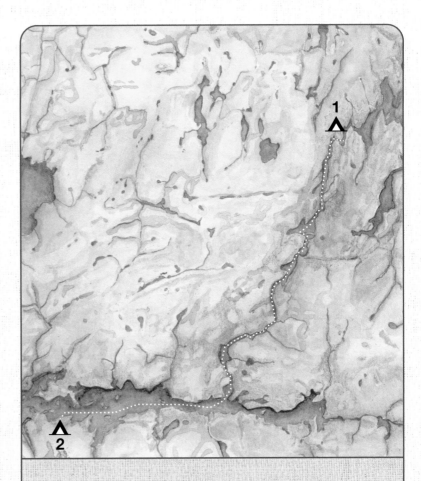

Journey from mikisiwaci to mistikopakitahawin

1. mikisiwaci (Eagle Hill)
2. mistikopakitahawin (Willow Fishing Place, name of a river by the camp that flows into Uhlman Lake where the people would set willow nets. From the words mistik (wood) and pakitahawin (fishing).

THE DURABILITY OF POTTERY

Pottery was an amazing invention that took people many years to perfect. Once that happened, thousands of years ago, the use and manufacture of pots spread across the boreal forest of Canada through people sharing this information with each other. After a clay pot is fired, it becomes a durable vessel that may also be waterproofed. Like modern dishes, some were broken accidentally from dropping them. They were often used for long periods of time, however, and passed on to other people. Pots were sometimes left in caches at camping locations, so that there would be vessels ready for the next time someone stopped there.

All of a sudden, from around the point, they saw the canoes pop out one by one. The men were paddling hard towards their families, knowing they were all in grave danger. As they hit the shore in their hurry, someone called out, "A rock has punctured a hole in one of our canoes!" Napiw called to his younger brother, "Nikik, fix this canoe as quickly as you can. We have to get going." Nikik walked over to the canoe and flipped it over. "No problem." While the others were loading, Nikik melted the necessary spruce gum, dried the area he was patching, prepared the birch patch, and made the canoe waterworthy again. He put the canoe into the water and grinned. "There! You have a canoe again."

When the last canoe was loaded and every person was safely inside, they paddled away from the danger that they could see coming towards them. Once they had escaped near-disaster, they set their canoes towards kinosi sākahīkan.

REPAIRING A CANOE

Birchbark canoes were made and used for millennia in northern Manitoba. They were a safe way to travel on the many waterways in the boreal forest, which provides all for its people. Canoes sometimes required repairs to the outer birchbark skin, to keep it waterproof. The seams were also treated with hot spruce or pine pitch applied with a stick. Paddlers re-applied this pitch almost daily to keep the canoe watertight. Since Amō's people were often travelling, they would need special kits with the necessary resin, pitch, spruce roots, panels of birch, and tools to apply patches in case those natural materials were not found at the next stop or during different seasons.

On page 11, the process of preparing birch tar for waterproofing utensils was described. Spruce or pine pitch used for canoe repair is different. The first step is to collect resin, which is sometimes found on the outside of the tree. Alternatively, a cut is made in the tree to collect the resin in a vessel. Then, it is heated over a fire and grease and charcoal are added. If the pitch mixture is too runny, it can melt in the summer heat, unsealing the canoe. If it is too thick, it can become brittle in the cold water and fall off. People developed the considerable skill set needed to respond to all of these variables through lived experience and through sharing.

SAP, RESIN, TAR, AND PITCH: SOME DEFINITIONS

Sap: the fluid, chiefly water with dissolved sugars and mineral salts, that circulates in the vascular system of a plant.

Resin: a thick, sticky substance, usually clear or translucent, in shades of yellow or brown, that oozes from various plants and trees. Natural resins are soluble in ether and alcohol, and are used in varnishes and lacquers.

Tar: Birch tar is made from heating the bark and collecting the liquid.

Pitch: Pitch is a black substance that is sticky when it is hot and very hard when it is dry. Pitch is used on the bottoms of boats and on the roofs of houses to prevent water getting in. It is prepared by mixing resin, charcoal, and fats.

ASINISKAW ĪTHINIWAK CLAN SYSTEM

The asiniskaw īthiniwak are born into ototimīhītowin, the group of your blood relatives, sometimes loosely called clans in English, which are determined by your mother's lineage. Each ototimīhītowin is represented by an animal, such as the bear or the wolf. By observing animals, the people learn important lessons for survival, such as what plants to eat or use as medicine, how to be good leaders or community members, and the attributes of their ototimīhītowin. Members of the mahīkanak minisiwin, the wolf family group, for example, are teachers, storytellers, and protectors. Wolf people were also good at hunting, travel, and raising children, and are seen as a model for social organization. Members of the masko minisiwin, the bear family group, are the medicine people and healers. Members of the moso minisiwin, or moose family group, are artists, inventors, and craftspeople. Asiniskaw īthinwak society is built on kinship relations between ototimīhītowin, minisiwin, and community members. In the past, women had important governance responsibilities such as selecting a leader. Leaders were chosen for their experience, expertise, and knowledge. Young people learned right behavior by observing community role models and continued to learn through apprenticeships as they grew older.

From late afternoon and all through the night they paddled, only stopping briefly a few times to rest, to drink water, and to eat a little food for energy. True to the spirit of the moswak, the Moose Family, they told stories and sang their old family songs as they paddled. The ones who did not paddle slept with the little children and woke up to take their turns while the tired paddlers grabbed a quick nap. The spirit was always strong. When they arrived at kinosi sākahīkan, dawn was barely breaking. They spread their sleeping robes and slept the deep sleep of exhaustion.

Midmorning, they awoke. In keeping with the ways of their camp, people resumed their work, laughing as they recounted the individual mishaps and adventures that had occurred in their escape from mikisiwi pawistik. That evening, a few of the men went hunting and returned joyously with two moose and the great news that the atīhkamikwak were running. There would be plenty of food to take them into the next season of takwākin.

Amid the great excitement about the fresh kills and the news of another great harvest, Nōcokīsīw told everyone to settle down. "There is still a lot of work to be done tomorrow to look after this meat. Today we will only catch enough atīhkamikwak for the evening meal. There will be plenty of food. Tomorrow there will be the minisiwin ceremony to acknowledge the apprenticeships coming up. Amō will be getting her askihko bundle and others will be given additional gifts for their existing bundles."

BUNDLES

There are many different kinds of bundles, including work bundles, ceremonial bundles, and medicine bundles. Work bundles contain special tools and other items used for specific tasks such as pottery making. Ceremonial bundles contain pipes or items for smudging and other ceremonies. Medicine bundles contain objects from important events in a person's life or the history of their family. For example, objects that have been given by loved ones who have passed away are often kept in those bundles. Medicine bundles are opened at certain times of the year when their owners will tell the story of how their bundle came to be. Bundles are sacred and are made throughout a person's life as they gather items with special meaning that come to them. Sapotawana, such as Amō's sapotawan, when she is recognized for her skill as a pottery maker, are often the occasion for a new item to be added to a bundle.

CREE VOCABULARY

askihko bundle: pottery-making bundle. This bundle would include all of the tools necessary to make pottery.

Night came, and Amō and Pīsim sat outside their mikiwāhp. For the first time in a while, they could see the stars and the moon. They both loved to watch the night skies. Others from the camp were sitting outside by their kotawāna, their campfires, happily visiting. Kisithinīw and Nōcokīsīw had their mikiwāhp beside Amō and Pīsim, and the girls could hear the old ones talking about the star people and how the stars had guided the asiniskaw īthiniwak in so many ways. There was so much more to learn about the gifts the people had received from the stars.

That night, everybody slept a peaceful sleep with no fear of fire. They dreamed of fresh moose meat and fish and the special minisiwin sapotawan ceremony that would come the next day.

USING THE STARS AS A NAVIGATION TOOL

For the asiniskaw īthiniwak, the stars are like a global positioning system or GPS. When people are very familiar with the land and the sky in their territory, at night they can use the stars for pinpointing where they are and where they are going. A person will point at a certain star and say, "You see that star there? Just below it is ithinisakahikan, Southern Indian Lake." This is how the people can get home safely at night, even when traveling in a boat going full speed—because the navigators know exactly where the land is, just by using the stars and their eyesight as a guide.

CEREMONIES

Ceremonies are performed for many reasons, such as to heal, to honour the dead, to learn and receive guidance, and more. Strict protocols, sets of rules that determine how a ceremony should be performed, are followed when conducting ceremonies. There are also important teachings connected to ceremonies and protocols, reasons for doing things that teach important lessons for how to live a good life. Each ceremony is different. Eating supper, for example, involves sitting down as a family and declaring an ancestor to be honored and remembered. Many ceremonies like this are an important way to keep the memory of one's ancestors alive, as it is believed that no one is truly dead until they are forgotten. Tobacco is an important part of many ceremonies and is often offered to the person who will lead the ceremony. Many ceremonies are performed under the guidance of an elder with the assistance of a helper, according to the elder's experience of how the ceremony should be performed. Elders learn how to conduct ceremonies by serving as helpers and apprentices themselves.

THE MISTĪKĪWAHP

A mistīkīwahp is a long lodge with doors on either end. It looks like two tepees joined together by a central lodge pole and is covered with spruce branches. The sides are made of poles made of thin tree trunks that are tied together to form a structure. Typically, this structure has two fire pits instead of one, as in other dwellings. A mistīkīwahp is used for holding community ceremonies or as a multi-family dwelling.

In the morning, they heard the robin's song welcoming them to the day once again. It took a moment for Amō to realize where she was and to remember what had happened yesterday.

"Wāniska, get up," Pīsim called to her from the other side of the mikiwāhp. "Let's go help kīkawinaw, our mother! We have to get ready for the ceremony!"

Soon all of them were up, working at the familiar tasks they remembered from previous sapotawan ceremonies. First, Nōcokīsīw was offered tobacco and moosehide to conduct the ceremony. Then the men worked at building the mistīkīwahp, the lodge where the ceremony would be held, and after that, they gathered wood for the kotawān. While this was happening, the women were making the meal for the feast. Each minisiwin also prepared their gifts for those who would be acknowledged at the ceremony.

Before they knew it, it was time to begin. Nōcokīsīw gathered everyone together around the ceremonial firepit. She said the opening prayers before kneeling to light the kotawān for the ceremony. Everyone stood in silent prayer until the kotawān was burning well. Amō tried to keep her mind on the prayers, but she fidgeted, wanting the time to go faster.

Then Nōcokīsīw began. She talked about how important the sapotawan is, not only for each person being honoured but also for the whole community.

"See Piponasiw here." She turned her gaze to Amō's little cousin, who beamed back at her. "He is two winters old. We celebrated his latest sapotawan this spring, when he had his walking-out ceremony. We were all overjoyed for him, because all of us are responsible for raising and guiding him. That is why our children's sapotawana are equally important for each and every one of us: because we raise our children together."

The people nodded their heads in agreement.

Nōcokīsīw went on: "Today we recognize Amō as she takes another step on that journey from a girl to a young woman, and we recognize her gifts as a pottery maker. Now if she ever breaks askihkwak again, she will be able to replace them with new ones!"

Everyone laughed.

Then she invited Amō to stand up. Amō stepped toward her, with her proud mom and dad following her. Tawipīsim presented a bundle to Nōcokīsīw, who turned and presented it to Amō.

"Nōsisim, my granddaughter, here are your tools to carry you on your journey in life as a pottery maker."

Amō already knew what would be in the bundle: pieces of hide for kneading and rolling the clay, a clamshell for smoothing it, a birchbark cup for carrying water, some fire-cracked rocks for tempering, a twisted cord bag, a collection of ocistasiyapiy, sinew, sticks, and small bones to decorate the pottery. She held it against her heart and then turned around and showed it to her mom and dad, smiling in gratitude. She noticed her sister Pīsim standing with the other members of the minisiwin, proudly smiling back at her.

When Amō and her parents joined the the minisiwin, her younger cousin Sakimīs leaned over to look at Amō's bundle and whispered, "I can't wait until I get my mīthikowisiwin, my special gift! Maybe it will be my turn in two more winters time."

After the formal opening, the young men started laying the food out on the ground, and everyone was served. The feast included sturgeon, moose meat, berries, pickerel, and atīhkamik. They ate and laughed and told stories for a long time, until their bellies were completely full. Then, as the sun was beginning to set, Kisithiniw led the atāmiskatowin, the gift-giving ceremony that followed. Everyone had gifts to give. Pīsim gave Amō a piece of the special red stone that was used for making beads. Nikik gave her a chert knife with a beautiful moosehide case. Tawipīsim gave her a kwakwāywat, beautifully decorated with an etching of a flower. Napiw gave her a small birch paddle that she could use to shape her pottery.

All the members of the mamawīwin, the gathering, came forward to offer their gifts to Amō. When the atāmiskatowin was finished, she had a little pile of gifts at her feet. "I'm blessed!" she said to herself. Blessed in osakihakana, loved ones, who honoured her on this day.

After the atāmiskatowin, everyone was ready to dance. "Haw, nimitān, let's celebrate!" Kisithiniw called. "Mwakwa, nikamō, sing!"

SPECIAL RED STONE

The special red rock that Pīsim gave Amō was red pipestone. A specific kind of red pipestone called catlinite has been quarried at the Pipestone National Monument in southwestern Minnesota for thousands of years and transported all over North America, and this piece likely came from there. It was used for making pipes, beads, pendants, and other decorative items. This red pipestone was an extraordinary gift to Amō since it had been traded or carried all the way north to ithinisakahikan, Southern Indian Lake. Red pipestone is also very similar to the colour of red ochre, which is another sacred mineral used by Indigenous people in Canada.

BIRCHBARK BASKET WITH ETCHING

Special kwakwāywat, like the one given to Amō, were sometimes decorated with etchings. These patterns are created by carefully cutting out the outer layer of the birchbark to make a contrasting section with that below. People used patterns such as flowers, animals, and other symbols that were important to them, their minisiwin, and their ototimīhītowin to decorate these special birchbark baskets. The exact meaning of the decorations is unknown, but we know that they were socially significant because the same patterns were used for about 2,500 years in northern Manitoba.

BIRCH PADDLE FOR SHAPING POTTERY

Wooden paddles, shaped from local birch branches, would likely have been used to create the smooth interiors and to thin the walls of the Late Woodland period pots that were manufactured inside fibre bags. This method would also have been used for earlier Middle Woodland pottery that was first created from coils and then smoothed with a paddle and stone anvil to refine the walls. Birch paddles, like their larger counterparts used in canoeing, are another example of gifts manufactured from that tree.

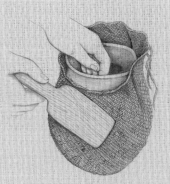

CHERT KNIFE

Indigenous people from northern Manitoba have been flintknapping, or making stone tools, for more than 9,000 years. They had to find the correct types of minerals and rocks that break by conchoidal fracture, a distinctive breaking pattern that enables sharp-edged, thin pieces to be produced by skilled knappers. These materials are known to be present at certain locations in Canadian Shield bedrock, but quartz, chert, and other suitable minerals are also found in glacially deposited sediments. As well, people traded for high-quality materials, such as Knife River chalcedony (from North Dakota), obsidian (from Wyoming and Washington), and others from very far away.

CREE VOCABULARY

atāmiskatowin: formal acknowledgment celebrating a person. This usually involves giving gifts. Today this is known as a give-away ceremony.

mamawīwin: A gathering for a specific reason, such as a feast time, the celebration of the birth of a baby, spring ceremonies, fall ceremonies, or midwinter ceremonies.

SUMMER CEREMONIES AND GATHERING PLACES

The asiniskaw īthiniwak were dispersed in small family groups for most of the year due to food availability. The summertime, however, meant warm weather and an abundance of options, particularly at good fishing locations such as mikisiwi pawistik. People gathered to share information, arrange marriages, harvest foods, and participate in ceremonies. Archaeological sites indicate that people used these excellent food-harvesting locales for many millennia. Some of them are still being used by modern asiniskaw īthiniwak, indicating an amazing continuity of knowledge in their traditional territory.

WĀWĀHTĪW

The asiniskaw īthiniwak believe that wāwāhtīw, the Northern Lights, are departed ancestors coming to dance for the people, acknowledging them, and showing that they are happy to be among their relatives. Sometimes they also bring messages. When a display of Northern Lights is over, you can say that you danced with your ancestors! The asiniskaw īthiniwak have a dance called pīcīsīmōwin, the round dance, which is very similar to the way the Northern Lights dance. The people have been taught not to whistle toward the Northern Lights because that would be disrespectful to the ancestors. Only those who have traveled a long way on their miskanaw have earned the respect to be able to whistle to the wāwāhtīw at special times.

The dancing went on long into the night, song after song. The people danced until the wāwāhtīw, the Northern Lights, came out. They moved together in the same rhythm as the spirits in the sky.

After a while, Amō stepped out of the dancing circle into the night, feeling the rush of energy through her body from the dancing and celebration. She stood beside the water and took in all the sensations of the night, watching the wāwāhtīw and the stars dancing around her. In the distance, she heard a loon calling. She thought about the ancestors who had made the sapotawan ceremony and had followed its teachings for thousands of years. She owed everything to them, and to the way of life that had enabled her people to thrive.

"I wonder what the future will bring?" she thought. "Will my relatives who come after me continue to practice our asiniskaw īthiniwak sapotawana?"

Three hundred and fifty winters have passed since that night. It is once again paskowī pīsim, the moulting moon, and the top of mikisiwi waci, Eagle Hill, is once more ripe with athoskanak, growing lush in the year after a big fire has burnt through the region. The berry pickers scramble up the hill excitedly, holding their buckets, looking at the big juicy athoskanak hanging down from the stalks. They race each other for the best spots in the patch.

Brother Lou walks behind the group, holding his paddle, looking at everything around him. He watches over the berry pickers to be sure they are safe. With his keen eye, he looks down and spots an odd-shaped rock in the burned soil at his feet. He kneels down and picks it up, and he realizes by its weight and colour that it is not a rock at all, but a piece of broken askihk. He turns it over and sees the designs left by his ancestors. This sherd of askihk in his hand was made many generations ago. He looks around his surroundings. "Nitotimak kaki nikanotīyik nimithotihan kīhtwam īnakiskātowāhk. My ancestors who have gone ahead, it is good to meet again."

We are in the era of aniskotapiwin, the reawakening of our connections with our ancestors. On this miskanaw, we are becoming nīhithaw again, spiritually, mentally, physically, and emotionally, mithwayāwin.

POTTERY DESIGN

Indigenous potters like Amō were taught skills for decorating vessels over many years. Each step of the process was transmitted from family members. The distinctive clay, manufacturing technique, shape, finish, and decorations were all chosen by the potter and reflected longstanding practices. In the area where Brother Lou found these sherds, and where Amō lived, the pots were decorated with punctates (round holes made with wood or bone tools) and sometimes with cord-wrapped sticks. These markings and patterns persisted for about 2,500 years in northern Manitoba.

CREE VOCABULARY

aniskotapiwin: strengthening of our connections with our ancestors and their teachings. Anisko means to add onto the strength of family, individual, and community. Aniskotapiw also means great-grandparents. This is connected to the idea of blood memory, because these connections are ingrained in us holistically from past generations.

nīhithaw: coming from the four directions. The directions correspond to different aspects of the self: physical, emotional, spiritual, and intellectual. When you embody all of the four directions it means you are holistically healthy in the way that you speak and act.

mithāwayāwin: to be in a good space, a positive state of being. Mithāw means good, and waway means the circle and also the idea of being whole. Mithāwayāwin means that you are able to use your gifts, because these gifts have been properly nurtured by your family and community.

49

Cree Glossary

akwayan (ah kwah yan) – tent for smoking food

aniskotapiwin (ah nee sko tah pee win) – strengthening connections with ancestors and their teachings

anoc ka nipihk (ah noch kah nee peek) – this summer

apiscithīnīwak (ah pis chi thee nee wuk) – little people

apwanāsk (up whan NAASK) – handmade tool made of willow or birch used for roasting fish over a fire

asiniskaw īthiniwak (uh si nee scow EE thi ni wuk) – Rocky Cree People

aski sakatask (us kee sah kah tusk) – cow parsnip

aski māskīkīya (us kee MAA SKEE KEE yah) – medicinal herbs

askihk (us kehk) – clay pot

askihko (us kee koh) – tools for making pottery

askihkwak (us kee wuk) – clay pots

atāmiskatowin (ah TAA mi skah toh win) – gift-giving ceremony for acknowledging a person

atīhkamik (ah TEE kah mihk) – whitefish run

atīhkamikwak (ah TEE kah mihk wuk) –whitefish

athoskanak (ah thoh skah nuk) – raspberries

awasis (ah wah sis) – child

iskwīsisak (is KWEE seh suk) – young girls

isohkistitat (eh soh kehs teh tut) – fresh water

ithinimina (eh thi neh meh nah) – blueberries

Ithinisakahikan (eh thin nee sah kah hey kun) – Southern Indian Lake

itī kāpasitīk (eh TEE KAA pah seh TEEK) – "A forest fire is there."

ītōmikathwāstik (EE TOH meh ka THWAAS tehk) – mirror calm

īwīthinohīt (EE WEE thin oh HEET) – skinned black bear; sacred ceremony for preparing bear carcass

kakānohkimowina (kah KAA noh keh moh weh nah) – a community's guiding principles

kakītiwi (kah KEE teh weh) – black or dark

kāmīkwaskwak (KAA MEE kwahs kwahk) – red-coloured sunset sky

kapasitihk (kah pah seh tehk) – forest fire

kasaskahānawak (kah sah ska HAA nah wuk) – the process of firing pottery

kīkawinaw (KEE kah weh now) – our mother (root word: nika, the first teacher)

kīhty amaya (KEE tee yah mah yah) – an elder

kinosiwi pimī (keh noh seh weh peh MEE) – fish oil

kinosi sākahīkan (keh noh seh SAH kah HEE kun) –Fish Lake (Uhlman Lake)

kisi aya (keh seh ah yah) – adult

kisithiniw Pipon (keh seh thi new pee pon) – the old man

kotawān (koh ta waan) – campfire; kotawāna – many campfires

kwakwāywata (kwa QUIY wah tu) – birchbark baskets

kwiskītīkī (kwee SKEE TEE KEE) – if the wind turns

mahīkanak minisiwin (mah HEE kah nuk) – wolf family group

mamawīwin (mah mah WEE win) – gathering

māskihkiwapwiy (MAA skeh keh wah pwey) – medicine tea

maskīhkiya (mah SKEE keh yah) – knowledge of medicine

māskīkīy (MAA SKEE KEEY) – medicine

masko minisiwin (mus ko meh neh seh win) – bear family group

maskwa (mus quah) – bear

mikisiwi pawistikōhk (meh keh seh weh pa weh steh KOHK) – Eagle Rapids

mikisiwi pawistik (meh keh seh weh pa weh stick) – Eagle Rapids

mikisiwi waci (meh keh seh weh) – Eagle Hill

mikiwāhp (meh keh WAAP) – dome-shaped dwellings made of trees growing in season or animal skins, often referred to as wigwams in English

minisiwin (meh neh seh win) – family group or clan

Misinipi (mih sih nih pi) – Big Water, specifically the Churchill River

miskanaw (meh skaa now) – one's individual life journey

mistīkīwahp (me STEE KEE wahp) – a long lodge, with doors on either end, made of bent poles covered with spruce branches with doors on either end

mithāwayāwin (me THAA wah YAA win) – to be in a positive state of being

mīthikowisiwin (MEE the koh weh seh win) – gift

mitihikan (meh te hee cun) – hand drum

moso minisiwin (moh soh meh neh seh win) – moose family group

moswak (mos wuk) – moose family

niciwām pawistik (neh chi WAAHM) – Brotherly Love Rapids

nīhithaw (NEE he thow) – coming from the four directions; corresponding to the physical, emotional, spiritual, and mental realms

nikāwī (neh KAA wee) – my mother

nimitān (neh meh TAAN)– let's dance

nīpin – summer

nipisiwata (nee pee see wut uh) – willow baskets

nitānis (neh TAAH nes) – my girl

nōhcawī (noh CHA wee) – uncle

ocistasiyapiy (oh chis tah tey hah pee) – sinew

onistamokiw (oh neh stah moh kew) – person in the front of the canoe

opahkwaci (oh pah kwah chi) – swim bladder, a gas-filled sac found in the body of some fish that controls buoyancy.

osakihakana (oh sa kee hah kah nah) – loved ones

oskatis (oh skah tes) – young adult

otakwahamo (oh tah kwah hah moh) – person at the back of the canoe

ototimīhītowin (oh toh teh mee hee toh win) – family group based on mother's lineage

otawīya (oh TAH wee yah) – her father

paskowī pīsim (pa skoh wee pee sim) – feather moulting moon

pīcīsīmōwin (pee chi see moh win) – round dance

pihcipothākan (peh che poh thaa cun) – fish weir (plural: pihcipothākana)

pīmikan (pee meh kahn) – preserved food composed of dried berries, dried moose or caribou, and fat

pimiwāta (peh meh waah tah) – fish oil containers

pitapan (pee tah pahn) – light is coming

sapotawan, sapotawana (sah poh tah wahn) – rite of passage, rites of passage

saska (sus kah) – to light a fire

takwākin (tah KWAH kin) – fall: takwā means gathering

thiwahikānik (thee wah he kaah nek) – pounded meat or fish

tisipicikana (teh seh peh chi kah nah) – food caches

wāhkotowin (WAH koh toh win) – adopted relatives

wāniska (WAH neh ska) – "Get up."

wapatānask(wah pah taah nahsk) – clay

wasipistān (wah seh peh staahn) – morning lark

waskatamo (wah ska tah moh) – water-lily root

wathaman (wah tha mahn) – clay with temper added used for making pottery

wāwāhtīw (waah waah tew) – Northern Lights

wihkaskwa (weh kah skwah) – wild mint

wihkaskwa (weh kah skwah) – mint tea

wīkis (WEE kis) – rat root

wīthin (wee thin) – animal fat

Story Contributors

◇◇

NISICHAWAYASIHK CREE NATION KNOWLEDGE KEEPERS

Carol Prince
Alma Spence
Christina Spence
Mona Hart
Natalie Spence
Henry Wood
Harry Spence
Larry Tait
Andrew Wood
Clifford Hart
Leroy Francois

O-PIPON-NA-PIWIN CREE NATION KNOWLEDGE KEEPERS

Bernard Dumas
Wilbur Wood
Thomas Spence

ASINISKAW ĪTHINIWAK MAMAWIWIN

Jennie Tait
Virginia Moose
Georgina Moodie
Larry Tait
Margaret Dumas
William Dumas

RESEARCHERS

Margaret Dumas
Warren Cariou
Mavis Reimer
Scott Hamilton
Roland Bohr
Doris Wolf
Linda DeRiviere
Jill Taylor-Hollings
Melanie Braith

RESEARCH ASSISTANTS

Alex Oldroyd
Melanie Belmore
Krystalyn Harms
Laura Gosse
Stephanie Skelton

ACKNOWLEDGEMENTS

Jen Storm
Emily Keijzer
Myra Sitchon
Kevin Brownlee
Leslie Baker
Arla Tait-Linklater
Fred Moose
Elvis Thomas
Clarence Surette
Chris McEvoy

Conseil de recherches en sciences humaines du Canada — Social Sciences and Humanities Research Council of Canada
Canadä

THE UNIVERSITY OF WINNIPEG

Nisichawayasi Nehetho Culture and Education Authority Inc.
NISICHAWAYASIHK CREE NATION

Nisichawayasihk Cree Nation
FAMILY AND COMMUNITY Wellness Centre

THE MANITOBA MUSEUM

Lakehead UNIVERSITY

Canada Council for the Arts — Conseil des arts du Canada

We acknowledge the support of the Canada Council for the Arts.
Nous remercions le Conseil des arts du Canada de son soutien.

HighWater Press gratefully acknowledges the financial support of the Province of Manitoba through the Department of Sport, Culture and Heritage and the Manitoba Book Publishing Tax Credit, and the Government of Canada through the Canada Book Fund (CBF), for our publishing activities.

HighWater Press is an imprint of Portage & Main Press.
Story-note illustration; map design: Alexis Cameron Ironside
Frontispiece map: Made from Natural Earth
Printed and bound in Canada by Friesens
Cover and interior design by Relish New Brand Experience

Library and Archives Canada Cataloguing in Publication

Title: Amō's sapotawan = Amō ōsapotawan / by William Dumas ; illustrated by Rhian Brynjolson.
Other titles: Amō ōsapotawan
Names: Dumas, William, 1949- author. | Brynjolson, Rhian, illustrator.
Description: Series statement: Six seasons series ; book two | Text in English with some text in Rocky Cree ("th" dialect of Cree).
Identifiers: Canadiana (print) 20220168628 | Canadiana (ebook) 20220169004 | ISBN 9781553799290 (hardcover) | ISBN 9781774920381 (EPUB) | ISBN 9781774920398 (PDF)
Subjects: CSH: First Nations—Canada—Social life and customs—Juvenile fiction. | LCGFT: Picture books.
Classification: LCC PS8607.U44318 A81 2022 | DDC jC813/.6—dc23

25 24 23 22   1 2 3 4 5

HIGHWATER PRESS

www.highwaterpress.com
Winnipeg, Manitoba
Treaty 1 Territory and homeland of the Métis Nation

Dedicated to Brother Lou

Louis Dumas was a third-generation land-keeper in the area where *Amō's Sapotawan* is set. He was our guide into the Eagle Rapids area, and he showed us the signs of asiniskaw īthiniwak ancestors on the land there, including the pottery sherds, the fish weir, and the place where the ancestors knapped chert to make arrowheads. Brother Lou was a residential-school survivor, but he escaped from school and found his healing out on the land. Although he has gone to the other side now, Brother Lou's dedication to preserving Rocky Cree history and traditions will live on. His knowledge and generosity have provided the inspiration for this story.

William Dumas, an asiniskaw īthiniw Knowledge Keeper and storyteller, was born in South Indian Lake, Manitoba. He has been an educator all his life and is passionate about Cree language and culture. William Dumas knows firsthand the power that storytelling has to teach Indigenous youth where they have come from and where they are going. He is the author of *Pīsim Finds Her Miskanaw*, the first book in the Six Seasons series, and of *The Gift of the Little People*, an illustrated short story for all ages (both published with Portage & Main Press). He lives in Thompson, Manitoba.

Rhian Brynjolson is a visual artist, author, book illustrator, and art educator. Rhian was awarded the Canadian Art Teacher of the Year in 2014. She is the author of *Teaching Art: A Complete Guide for the Classroom*, and has illustrated fifteen children's books. Rhian has worked with the River on the Run artist collective, making and performing art to raise awareness of environmental concerns affecting the Lake Winnipeg watershed. Rhian lives and works on the edge of Treaty 3 territory, in the boreal forest of eastern Manitoba. Her work is currently exhibited as part of the Virtual Water Gallery online exhibit https://gwf.usask.ca and at https://www.rhianbrynjolson.com/